## HELLO...

Jim's blond with blue eyes and is six feet tall . . . .
He told Angie so himself.

Angie's five feet tall, thin, and also has blonde hair and blue eyes . . . .

That's how she described herself to Jim.

But Jim and Angie have never actually seen each other.

They've only spoken on the phone.

Could there be more here than meets the eye — or the ear?

**Other Scholastic Paperbacks
you will enjoy:**

*Dear Lovey Hart, I am Desperate*
  by Ellen Conford

*Do You Love Me, Harvey Burns?*
  by Jean Marzollo

*Girl Meets Boy*
  by Hila Colman

*Halfway Down Paddy Lane*
  by Jean Marzollo

*If This Is Love, I'll Take Spaghetti*
  by Ellen Conford

*Sarah Bishop*
  by Scott O'Dell

*A Smart Kid Like You*
  by Stella Pevsner

*When We First Met*
  by Norma Fox Mazer

# Hello... Wrong Number

# Hello... Wrong Number

## Marilyn Sachs

SCHOLASTIC INC.
New York Toronto London Auckland Sydney

ISBN 0-590-44504-9

Text copyright © 1981 by Marilyn Sachs. Illustrations copyright © 1981 by Pamela Johnson. All rights reserved. This edition published by Scholastic Inc., 730 Broadway, New York, NY 10003, by arrangement with E.P. Dutton, Inc.

12 11 10 9 8 7 6 5 4 3 2          2 3 4 5/9

Printed in the U.S.A.          01

*for Ann Durell*

# Hello... Wrong Number

# Monday night

The telephone rang.

"Hello!" said the boy.

"Hello!" came the girl's voice. "Is this Jim?"

"Yes?"

"Jim, this is Angie."

"Who?"

"Angie Rogers. Betty Lyons's friend. I met you at her party Saturday night."

"I don't . . . ."

"Listen! I know you were sore because I . . . I got upset when we were dancing. I just want to say I was wrong. I'm sorry."

Look, I . . . ."

"I mean, I didn't know you very well. That's why I got upset. But I like you. I'd like to go dancing with you. How about this Saturday night?"

"No, you don't understand."

"Yes, I do understand. You're angry because I told you to stop. You think I'm some kind of prude. I'm not, Jim. I'm really not. But I just didn't know you very well. You came on too fast."

"But I'm not him."

"What do you mean? Isn't this Jim?"

"Yes, I'm Jim. But not the Jim you want."

"Isn't this Jim McCone?"

"No."

"Isn't this 527-3701?"

"No, it's 527-3761."

"Oh my God!"

She hung up.

# Monday night —
## a little later

"**H**ello!"

"Hello, Jim?"

"Yes. Who's this?"

"This is . . . the girl who called about half an hour ago."

"Oh, yes."

"Listen. I don't know who you are. But I said some things I wouldn't want to get around."

"I don't know who you are either."

"But you sound like somebody about my own age. Do you go to Washington High School?"

"Yes, but it's a pretty big place."

3

"Maybe so, but everybody knows who Jim McCone is."

"Oh, him!"

"See! You do know who he is."

"But I don't know who you are."

"I told you my name before."

"I only remember the Angie. I don't remember the rest of it."

"That's good. I don't want you to know the rest of it. But promise you won't tell him."

"Tell him what?"

"What I just said about him before."

"Why should I tell him?"

"I don't know. But promise you won't."

"There's nothing to tell."

"Oh yes there is. I don't want him to know what I said because I decided I'm not going to go through with it."

"That's good."

"He's got such a swelled head. All the girls in the school are after him. He thinks he's so great. He thinks he can put his hands all over you the first time you dance with him. I hate him."

"He sure is one fatheaded jerk."

"What do you know, anyway?"

"I thought you just said you hated him."

"I do. And I hate myself too for liking him. I've been sitting here for hours thinking about what I was going to tell him. I've been saying it over and over again in different kinds of voices. Isn't that stupid? Me apologizing to him because he was fresh."

"Why should you?"

"Because he's so great. He's the best-looking kid in school. And he's such a great dancer. I think he's even better looking than John Travolta."

"Yuk!"

"All year I've been trying to get him to notice me. I've done everything. I smile at him whenever we pass in the hall. I try to kid around with him during lunch. I know where all his classes are and I hang around outside. I even know where he lives. Sometimes I walk by his house, hoping he'll come out and see me."

"I think he's a nerd."

"He is. But finally I went to this party Saturday night because I knew he was going to be there. I even bought a new red skirt for it. He asked me to dance. But then he started doing things I didn't like. I could have made a joke of it. But I got mad and said, 'Bug off!' So he did. He danced with Sue Follett the rest of the evening."

"I'm glad you told him off."

"I'm not. So then I thought I could call him tonight and make it up. So, wouldn't you know! My luck! I go ahead and blow it. I get a wrong number. I always make that mistake with the zero in a telephone number."

"Maybe it's just as well."

"I don't think so. Now I don't have the courage."

"Maybe you didn't really want to call him. Maybe that's why you dialed the wrong number. Maybe deep down in your mind you said to yourself, I don't really want to dial his number. I don't really want to talk to him. He's the biggest jerk who ever lived. Why should I call him? Why should I apologize to the biggest jerk who ever lived?"

"What business is it of yours who I call and who I apologize to?"

"None at all."

"I can apologize to anybody I like."

"Sure you can. If you want to make a Prize

A jerk of yourself, go right ahead. He'd probably only laugh in your face anyway. He despises women. He just uses them."

"That's none of your goddamned business."

"You're absolutely right. Why don't you just bug off and stop bothering me?"

The boy hung up.

# Tuesday night

"**H**ello!"
    "Jim?"

"Oh God! Not you again!"

"Yeah, it's me. Look, I'm sorry. I didn't mean to fight with you."

"Fine, let's just forget the whole thing."

"That's what I want. For you to forget the whole thing."

"I told you that's what I want too."

"Great! And just one other thing. Please, don't hang up yet. Just promise you won't tell him."

"I told you I'm not going to tell him."

"But promise."

"Look, can you see me going up to him and

8

saying, 'Oh Jim, I just want you to know. This dumb girl, Angie something, called me up last night and said it was fine with her if you did anything you like with her. Just give her a ring and she'll fall right down at your feet.' "

"You liar. I never said that."

"Look, will you leave me alone? Why do you keep bothering me anyway?"

"All I want is for you to promise."

"Okay, okay, I promise."

"Thanks a lot, Jim. I'm sorry I bothered you. I really am, and I promise never to call you again, either. I know I've been a pest but I really don't want him to know what I was going to do."

"You're right. You won't be sorry."

"I hope I won't."

"No, you won't. You'll get over him. It's like kicking a bad habit. He'd only make you miserable anyway. I know what he's like. He was always a louse."

"How long have you known him?"

"Since fourth grade. He used to cheat. All through junior high he cheated. A couple of times he got caught. Once he failed French because he cheated. The teacher made his mother come in. Even then he used to get girls to do his homework and let him copy from them. Sometimes they got into trouble and he'd act innocent. I used to tell him, 'You're the most slimy, disgusting rat I know!' "

"You told Jim McCone that?"

"I sure did. I told him lots of other things too."

"What did he say? What did he do?"

"Oh, he takes it from me. He wouldn't dare do anything to me. He's scared of me. I'm not one of those silly, dumb girls who like to be abused."

"Say, what's your name, anyway?"

"What's your name?"

"I told you already."

"But I forgot."

"Well, I don't want you to know my whole name."

"Why not?"

"Oh, just in case."

"In case what?"

"Just in case you decide to tell him."

"But I just promised you I wouldn't."

"Well, maybe it's just as well you don't

know who I am. I told you some things that are kind of embarrassing."

"Okay. So maybe I don't want you to know my name either."

"Who cares?"

"That's right. Who cares?"

"Well, I guess I better say good-night."

"Good night."

# Wednesday night

"**H**ello!"
    "Hello, Jim?"
  "No, just a minute."
  "Hello!"
  "Hello, Jim? Who was that?"
  "My brother. Who's this?"
  "It's Angie."
  "I was afraid it was you."
  "I know. I'm being such a pest, but I'm in real trouble."
  "Trouble? What kind of trouble?"
  "In my head mostly. I saw him in school today. He looked so cute. He wore . . . ."
  "Who did you see?"

"Him. Jim. Jim McCone. I couldn't help myself. I felt weak all over. I got prickles in the back of my neck. And I began to sweat."

"What did I ever do to deserve this?"

"He acted like he didn't see me, but I could see he was watching me. I can feel it — sort of an electric shock. I know he's interested in me. All I have to do is call him up. I know he'd say yes. I've been sitting here thinking about calling him. I've had to hold on to my right hand to stop myself. I don't want to call him. I know he's a louse and conceited and he means trouble. But I'm afraid I'm losing control. I'm afraid I'm going weak in the knees. Then I thought of you."

"Thanks a lot."

"I thought of you, Jim, because I know you're honest. I know you don't like him. I thought I'd call you and listen to all the bad things you know about him. Please help me, Jim."

"I can't believe this is really happening to me."

"Go ahead, Jim. Tell me some bad things about him."

"You know, I just might have other things to do."

"I'm sorry."

"Maybe you can sit around shooting the bull all night but I haven't got the time."

"What do you have to do?"

"Lots of things. I have an English exam tomorrow, and I have to read thirty pages of this dumb book."

"What dumb book?"

"*The Old Man and the Sea*. Then I have to change the washer in the kitchen faucet. The faucet keeps dripping and I promised my mother I would fix it."

"Why can't your father do it?"

"Because he doesn't know how. He's a real goof-off. When he's home all he does is sit in front of the TV and drink beer. He doesn't talk to anybody, much less fix anything."

"Sounds like my father."

"He likes to complain though. If anybody's talking or laughing or singing, he complains."

"Does your mother sing?"

"No, she doesn't."

"So who sings?"

"Well — I do."

"You sing?"

"Yes, I sing."

"No kidding. You really sing?"

"So what?"

"But that's great. You have a nice voice. I mean, just speaking to you I can tell. I love music — especially The Bee Gees and K.C. and the Sunshine Band."

"They're okay."

"What kind of songs do you sing?"

"I write my own."

"No kidding!"

"Yeah. I write my own."

"That's just great. I know somebody else who writes songs and sings them. Kathy Snyder. She has a fantastic voice. Do you know her? Kathy Snyder?"

"No."

"She's in the chorus. She does a lot of solo numbers. Are you in the chorus?"

"No."

"How come?"

"They don't do the kind of stuff I like. All they do is that 'Jingle Bells' kind of stuff. I don't have the time for that kind of junk."

"But she's good. And they let her do her

own things. Didn't you ever go to any of their concerts?"

"No. I'm not interested in amateurs."

"Amateurs? Aren't you an amateur?"

"No . . . I'm a pro."

"You mean you make money singing?"

"Sure I do. Maybe not a lot. But I've been getting more and more work."

"All by yourself?"

"Sometimes. Sometimes with a group."

"Do you play anything?"

"Electric guitar."

"No kidding!"

"Look, I've really got a lot to do. I don't want to be mean, but I think you have to work out your problems by yourself."

"I'm trying. I really am."

"I don't know you, of course, but you sound like an okay person."

"No I don't. I guess I sound like a real pest to you. I guess I really am a pest to you."

"It's okay. Forget it."

"I'm not like this most of the time. Most of the time I'm pretty cool. I don't go blowing my lid. Except when it comes to Jim McCone. When it comes to him I go crazy."

"So what do you need it for?"

"That's what I keep telling myself. Plenty of guys are interested in me. I never have trouble finding a boyfriend. I've had four since I started high school."

"That's a lot."

"And a few in between that didn't really count. But what I feel for Jim McCone is different. It's heavy. For the past couple of years I've been crazy about him. Even while I had all those other guys I kept thinking about him. I kept thinking if he liked me I'd give them all up for him."

"He changes girl friends every month."

"I know he does. But I keep thinking it would be different with me. I would understand him."

"What's to understand? He's a creep."

"Ah!"

"A real weirdo creep. He's a lousy friend. He borrows money and never pays it back. He picks his nose in front of people. He thinks he's a real classy dude because he has more clothes than anybody else, and his mother has to work at two jobs to pay for them. He doesn't have an idea in his head. All he thinks

17

about is himself if he thinks at all. I tell him all the time what a weirdo creep he is. And he's only interested in girls as sex objects. Is that what you want to be — a sex object?"

"Thanks, Jim. Thanks a lot."

"For what?"

"For helping me. I'm going to try to get over him. I'm really going to try."

"You can do it. Keep your mind on other things."

"Thanks, Jim."

"It's all right."

"Good night, Jim."

"Good night."

# Thursday night

"**H**ello!"

"Hello, Jim?"

"Angie?"

"See. You know who I am already."

"Only your voice, Angie. I'd know your voice anywhere."

"Why is that?"

"Well—it's an unusual voice."

"What's unusual about my voice?"

"Nothing. Nothing. Forget it."

"No. I want to know what you meant. What did you mean when you said you'd know my voice anywhere?"

"Well . . . it's just that your voice is . . . well . . . different."

19

"What do you mean different? Are you laughing? I think you're laughing. I think you're laughing at me."

"I'm not laughing. I mean, I'm not really laughing . . . not at you . . . I'm just . . . ."

She could hear him making funny, choked-up sounds. She knew he was laughing at her. She didn't like it when people laughed at her, especially people she didn't know. She felt like crying. She felt like yelling at him and making him stop.

"Drop dead!" she yelled, and she hung up.

# Thursday night —
# fifteen minutes later

"**H**ello!"
    "Hello."

"Look Angie, I'm sorry I made you feel bad. I didn't mean to make you feel bad. I would have called you back and apologized, but I didn't have your number."

No answer.

"Angie?"

No answer.

"Look, I know you're there. I can hear you breathing. Have you got a cold or something? You're breathing very loud."

"No, I'm not breathing loud. I'm chewing my fingernails. I always chew my fingernails when I'm nervous."

"So anyway, Angie, I'm sorry. Okay?"

"No, it's mean to laugh at somebody for something they can't help."

"I know. I'm sorry."

"People always laugh at my voice. Because it's so squeaky. They used to call me Minnie Mouse in elementary school. Even then people laughed at me."

"You shouldn't let it bother you."

"It's easy to say that if you don't have something wrong with you. What have you got wrong?"

"I . . . I . . . I . . . ."

"See. You probably don't have anything wrong."

"Everybody has something wrong."

"I just bet you don't. You have a great voice. I can hear that — a real deep, gorgeous voice. I bet you're good-looking too. I bet you're tall and dark and handsome. Right?"

"No, I'm not. I'm . . . I'm blond."

"See. And I bet you've got big, blue eyes."

"Well, they're blue."

"And I bet people don't laugh at you."

"I don't let anybody laugh at me."

"See — you can make them scared of you,

too. The way you do with Jim McCone. If you can say anything to him and get away with it, you can get away with it with anybody. But it's not so easy with me. I'm small. I hate being small. My girl friend, Betty Lyons, she says she wishes she was small. She's about five foot seven and she's really stacked. But she's on a diet all the time. Me, I can eat anything I like and I stay the same. I'm little and flat as a pancake. I want to be tall and important."

"You can still be important even though you're small."

"No you can't. When you're small you feel small. You act small. Everybody says I'm so cute. But who wants to be cute? Nobody takes me seriously. I want people to take me seriously."

"Everybody wants to be something they're not."

"What do you want to be, Jim?"

"Me? I want to be a rock singer."

"But you are one already. You're only a kid. You sound like you're my age — sixteen and a half — and already you're a pro. How old are you anyway?"

"Me? I'm . . . I'm . . . seventeen."

"I'm going to be seventeen in March. When's your birthday?"

"In October."

"You're a junior too, aren't you?"

"Uh huh."

"Whose homeroom?"

"Nope."

"What do you mean, 'Nope'?"

"I'm not telling you."

"Why not?"

"Because . . . just because."

"Because you don't want me to know who you are. Because you think I'm going to hang around your homeroom and bother you. You think I'm going to come and tell you all my troubles. You think . . . ."

"Angie."

He could hear funny sounds over the line. Noisy, choking sounds.

"Angie?"

No answer, but the sounds continued. Then he began laughing because he knew she was laughing. It was always better when two people could share the laughter. Finally, she spoke.

"You know, you're right. I probably would

be bothering you if I knew who you were. I'd come to you with all my problems. And besides, maybe I don't want you to know who I am."

"Why not?"

"Oh — because I like talking to you. I like telling you things I would never tell anybody else. Like the way I feel about Jim. And the way I feel about myself. And the way . . . well . . . other things."

"What other things?"

"Let's save it for another time."

"Okay. But you're not mad?"

"No, I'm not mad. How can you be mad at somebody you don't even know? How can you be mad at a voice?"

"That's right."

"Good night, Jim."

"Good night, Angie."

# Friday night—
## early

"Hello!"
"Hello Jim."
"Hello Angie."
"Are you busy?"
"No, it's okay. I just finished dinner. Wait! I just want to take one more bite out of this doughnut. Mmm. There. But you're early. How come you're so early?"
"Because it's Friday."
"So?"
"I figured you'd be busy. I wanted to get you before you left."
"Oh — that's right. Are you going out someplace tonight, Angie?"
"Yes. I'm going dancing."

"Who are you going with?"

"Oh, with a bunch of other kids. Nobody important. Just a bunch of kids who like to dance. Do you like to dance, Jim?"

"Me? Sure . . . I like to dance."

"Where do you generally go?"

"Me? Oh . . . lots of places."

"Do you ever go to the place on Lincoln?"

"Sure."

"Or to Floaters on Union?"

"Sure."

"Maybe you've seen me."

"Maybe."

"Maybe you've even danced with me. Wouldn't that be funny, Jim, if you danced with me and didn't know it? Wouldn't that be something?"

"Most of the time I'm busy singing."

"Tonight?"

"Yeah, tonight."

"Where?"

"Oh, a little place. Just a coffee shop. Just a little place. They don't pay much, but I know the owner. I'm doing him a favor."

"Are you doing it yourself or with a group?"

"Tonight? With a group."

27

"How big a group?"

"How big? Three. Three of us. Another guy, me, and a girl."

"What do they do?"

"The guy plays the drums and the girl . . . she sings too. And she plays a guitar."

"Is she good?"

"Pretty good."

"Is she . . . your girl friend?"

"No. We're strictly professional."

"I guess it's better that way. But Jim, I wanted to ask you something. I wanted to ask you yesterday, but I didn't. There's so many things to say when I talk to you. I forget half of them."

"That's funny."

"It really is. You're so easy to talk to. I never met a guy who was as easy to talk to as you."

"You never met me either."

"Maybe that's why. Maybe if we met each other we wouldn't be able to say a single word. Maybe we'd hate each other."

"Maybe we wouldn't even notice each other. That would be even worse. But what did you want to ask me, Angie?"

"Oh — that's right. You know — I guess it was on Wednesday — you said I should keep my mind on other things. You said if I wanted to get over Jim McCone I should keep my mind on other things."

"That's right. You should."

"Well, that's what I want to ask you. What other things?"

"Are you kidding?"

"No. I mean it."

"Well, I don't know what other things. What are you interested in?"

"I'm interested in dancing."

"So keep your mind on dancing."

"But that doesn't work. Because I need a guy when I dance, and I keep thinking that nobody dances like Jim McCone."

"Well, what else are you interested in?"

"I can't think of anything else."

"What kind of hobbies do you have?"

"I don't have any hobbies."

"Didn't you say you liked music?"

"I do. I love music."

"Well, listen to music. Do you know Pink Floyd or Jefferson Starship? There's a whole bunch of great records you can listen to."

"But music makes me think of . . . well . . . love. And if I think of love, I end up thinking about Jim. You see, it's a problem. I can't listen to too much music. That wouldn't be a good idea."

"I can't figure you, Angie."

"What do you mean?"

"I just can't figure if you're not making this all up. If you're not just putting me on."

"Why?"

"Because sometimes you sound so . . . so . . . ."

"So . . . what?"

"I'm trying to find the right word."

"I'm waiting."

"Now don't get sore, but sometimes you really sound kind of . . . kind of young."

"I'm going to be seventeen in March."

"I know. But when you say things like what should you think about to stop thinking about Jim . . . well . . . ."

"Well what?"

"Well, it sounds kind of silly, to tell you the truth. How do I know what you should think about? It's a funny question to ask somebody you don't even know."

"I don't think it's such a funny question."

"Well, suppose I asked you. Suppose I said I was trying to get over some girl. Suppose I asked you what I should think about. What would you tell me?"

"I'd tell you to get out more. I'd tell you not to sit home and think about her. I'd tell you to avoid her. If she goes to your school, I'd tell you to go the other way if you see her coming down the hall. I'd tell you to join some clubs, meet some new people, go out with some other girl. I'd tell you to go swimming or bowling or skiing or skating in the park. I'd tell you to tell yourself to just stop. To make up your mind, That's it, kid. No more. She's not worth it."

"So there you are. That's just great."

"See. It's not such a funny question."

"Okay. But you answered it. Better than I could. You didn't have to ask me. You already knew."

"That's right. I guess I did."

"You need to have a little more confidence, Angie. I think that's your real problem."

"Do you really think so?"

"I think you have to have more faith in

31

yourself. You've got a good head. I mean, I think you have a good head. You don't have to be silly and insecure."

"That's true. I'm very insecure."

"Why should you be?"

"Maybe because I'm so small."

"How small are you anyway?"

"I'm just five feet."

"That's not so small for a girl."

"It's small for anybody. Everybody towers over me. I'm the smallest one in the family. My parents are both average and my sisters are both taller than me. Even my little sister, Dinah. She's only fourteen and she's five foot four already."

"Forget about being small. It's what you are inside that counts."

"It's easy for you to say that. You're so tall. How tall are you, anyway?"

"Me? Oh . . . about six feet."

"See. Everybody's bigger than me, and all of them put me down."

"All of who?"

"My family. Nothing I ever do is right."

"But you've got friends, don't you? And

you said the other night you always can attract boys."

"Yeah, it's easy for me. But . . . but . . . ."

"But what?"

"But even there . . . they think because I'm little and I guess kind of cute that I'm just a silly blonde. Even you said I was silly."

"I never said that. I just said sometimes."

"Well, if you saw me you'd think I was all the time, because I look so small and maybe helpless."

"Maybe it's your fault."

"My fault!"

"I mean because you act like that."

"You think I do it on purpose? You think I say to myself, Okay, Angie, look up at that dumb boy as if he is Superman. Make the jerk feel big and important next to silly, little me. Just don't let him see how smart you really are. And how angry. Because boys make you act so silly. Because it's their fault. And maybe it's not their fault. Maybe it's my fault. Maybe I don't have to play that kind of game. Maybe I'll like myself better if I don't."

"Wow!"

"What happened to me? I don't know what happened to me."

"You're really something."

"I never said anything like that before to anybody. I never even said it to myself."

"Angie, you know something, Angie?"

"What?"

"You don't need to come to me for advice. Maybe I should try coming to you."

"I never give you a chance. I keep going on and on. I don't really know anything about you. It's my fault. I have to shut up. We have to talk about you."

"Another time."

"That's right, Jim, another time."

"Have fun tonight, Angie."

"You too, Jim."

"Good night."

"Good night."

# Monday night

"**H**ello!"
"Hello Jim."

"Angie? What happened to you?"

"Nothing happened to me. Why?"

"Well, you didn't call Saturday and you didn't call Sunday."

"I figured you needed the weekend off."

"Oh!"

"You mean you missed me?"

"Well . . . ."

"Come on, Jim. I think you missed me."

"Okay, okay. I missed you."

"Hey, that's great. I wanted to call. I really did. I kept thinking about you. I have so many things to tell you. But I said no. He's busy. He doesn't want me to bother him."

"No, Angie. You don't bother me. I like hearing from you. Keep on calling."

"Every day?"

"Sure. Unless you're busy."

"Well, even if I am busy I can always call. We have unlimited calls. I also have my own phone. I mean, my sisters and I have our own phone. Pat doesn't use it much. She's nineteen. She goes to City College. She studies all the time. My parents act like she's the only one in the family. They're so proud of her they could burst."

"Why are they so proud of her?"

"Because she's smart. She wants to be an accountant, or maybe even a lawyer. She's always gotten good marks. They're always on me about her. 'Why can't you be more like your sister?' 'Why don't you study the way Pat does?' 'Why don't you change your ways?' 'Why don't you just stop being you?'"

"They always like the oldest one best. I have an older sister too."

"You have a brother too, right?"

"Yes. He's younger than me. He's fifteen.

And then I have a younger sister, Ellen. She's eight. She's a brat. Nobody can stand her. My mother spoils her rotten."

"It's lousy being in the middle. You're in the middle too, just like me. We have a lot in common."

"My father is the worst. I don't mind anybody else. Only him."

"My father's not so bad. I think maybe if my mother didn't keep pushing him, he'd get off my back. I think he really likes me. I used to think he liked me the best but . . . see, there I go again."

"What do you mean?"

"I mean, there I go again talking about myself. I don't want to keep talking about myself. I want to talk about you. I mean, I want you to talk about you. Go ahead."

"Go ahead what?"

"Go ahead and talk about yourself."

"Come on, Angie, cut it out. I can't just start talking about myself. I'm not a TV set. You can't just turn me on and off."

"Okay, okay, don't get sore. You've got a temper, don't you?"

"So do you."

"Something else we have in common. Anyway, you were talking about your father. What were you saying about your father?"

"I can't stand him."

"Your father?"

"Yes, my father. I can't stand him and I wish I could move out of here and never come back."

"What's he like?"

"He's a loudmouth, a real bull. He thinks he's the only one who lives here. If he wants a beer, he wouldn't think of getting up from in front of the TV set. He'll just holler out to my mother. He has her running back and forth all night long, bringing him things. She's a real slave."

"Why does she do it?"

"Because she's a nut. I mean, she's not a bad person, but sometimes she gets so tired waiting on him hand and foot, she takes it out on the rest of us. Mostly me. My father likes to see my mother get mad. He starts laughing. The whole room shakes. He's a big guy — six foot three and all fat. Talk about being small and unimportant. He's big and fat and

38

noisy and the most unimportant man who ever lived."

"It doesn't sound like you like him."

"Like him! I just told you. I can't stand him. And he can't stand me either. When he's home I can't practice. He can have the TV set going full blast, but he can't stand hearing me play or sing."

"So what do you do?"

"I have to do it when he's not around. Or on a weekend if my mother can ever drag him out somewhere."

"I guess you can rehearse with your friends."

"What friends?"

"Those two in your group."

"Yeah . . . that's right . . . I can practice with them. But it's not the same."

"That's a shame. Isn't he proud of you?"

"For what?"

"For performing the way you do. Most kids your age don't get jobs the way you do."

"He wouldn't care if I was Fleetwood Mac. He has no interest in music. Not only rock — all kinds."

"What kind do you do?"

"Mostly rock . . . a little country once in a while."

"Say, Jim . . . ."

"What?"

"Well, I know this sounds funny but . . . ."

"What?"

"I'd love to hear one of your songs. Would you play me one?"

"You mean over the phone?"

"Sure."

"Aah . . . it's not the same."

"Well, I know that. Just like hearing a tape isn't the same as hearing the performer in person. But it's better than nothing. Come on, Jim."

"You really want to hear one of my songs?"

"I really do. I've been wanting to ask you."

"Well . . . ."

"Come on, Jim."

"Okay, but I'll have to do it low. My old man is downstairs, hooked up to the boob tube. If he hears me he'll raise the roof."

"Anyway you like, Jim."

"Maybe I'll get my guitar. Hang on, Angie."

"I sure will."

She could hear him rustling around on the other side of the line. She could hear him tuning up his guitar. It was exciting. Finally he picked up the phone again.

"Hello, Angie?"

"Yup. I'm still here."

"Okay. Look. I'll play you one of my older songs. I wrote this one more than a year ago. It's not all that good but I know it pretty well. Lately I've been doing some more complicated ones."

"Okay Jim. Go ahead."

"I'm going to put the phone down, and I'll try to get close to it so you won't lose the sound."

"Okay."

She heard a few twangs, and then he began to sing. His voice faded a little from time to time. But she could hear every word of the song.

Out in the rain, out in the storm
Winter winds drive me — all alone.
I think of you, babe, warm and kind.

Those old days were best.
Those old days are gone.

Think of me, babe,
Sometimes when you're blue.
Think of a guy who ever was true.
Think of a friend out in the storm.
Think of the times, lost but still warm.

He made rain and storm sounds on his guitar. For the last few lines of the song, he played on one string. It sounded sad and lonely. She waited a few seconds when he stopped singing. She could hear him breathing quickly on the other side of the phone. She said softly, "Jim."

"Yes?"

"Jim — that was so beautiful — so sad."

"That's a quiet one. I don't know why I picked that one. Most of the others are faster and jumpier."

"But Jim, it was beautiful."

"Really?"

"I loved it, Jim. And your voice! You have such a wonderful voice."

"No kidding?"

"I thought you'd have a deeper voice when you sang, but it's not deep at all. It's beautiful. You sound like Elton John."

"I can sing deeper. Sometimes I sing deeper."

"But it's a wonderful song — a wonderful, beautiful song. I can't believe you wrote it."

"I did it a year ago. But you're the only one who ever heard it."

"How come? Didn't you ever sing it on one of your appearances?"

"Oh . . . no . . . well, no, I never have. It's sort of a special song. It's sort of personal."

"You should sing it in front of an audience, Jim. They'd really love it. You're really talented."

"You mean it?"

"I wouldn't kid you about something like that. One thing, Jim, I'm honest. I always tell the truth. I have plenty of faults, but a liar I'm not. I'm honest, Jim, just like you."

"Just like me?"

"And you're good, Jim. You're really good."

"Thanks, Angie. It means a lot to me to have you think so. Angie?"

He could hear somebody talking to her.

43

Even though she must have put her hand over the receiver, he could hear her say, "Can't you get off my back!" There were some angry voices going on for a while. And then she came back.

"Jim."

"Yes?"

"Look, I've got to go now. My mother's on me again for a change. But I wish I could stay and listen to you sing."

"Another time, Angie."

"That's right, Jim. We'll have lots of time."

"Good night, Angie."

"Good night."

# Tuesday night

"**H**ello!"

"Hello. Is Jim there?"

"No he isn't. Who's this?"

"This is a friend of his. Angie. Uh, when will he be back?"

"He should be back in an hour or so. Do you want him to call you back?"

"No, that's all right. I . . . I don't know where I'll be. If you wouldn't mind just telling him Angie called and I'll call back."

"I'll tell him."

"Thank you very much."

"Good-bye."

# Tuesday night —
## an hour and a half later

"Hello!"

"Hello, Jim?"

"No, this is Ellen."

"Oh, Jim's little sister."

"Yeah. Who's this?"

"A friend of Jim's."

"Do I know you?"

"No. I don't think so."

"How did you know I was Jim's little sister?"

"I guess he told me."

"What's your name?"

"Angie."

"Angie what?"

"Look, Ellen, is Jim there? I'd like to talk to Jim."

"No. He's not here."

"Okay. Well, could you give him a message?"

"Wait until I get a pencil. Okay, what's the message?"

"Could you tell him please that Angie called, and I'll call him tomorrow about 8:30."

"Wait. . . . I'm writing. . . . Angie called. . . . How do you spell Angie?"

"A-N-G-I-E."

"Okay. Wait until I get it all down."

"I'm waiting."

"Didn't you call before?"

"Yes, I did."

"My mother said you did. She said she didn't know who you were. Are you Jim's girl friend?"

"No. We're just friends."

"I'm glad you're not his girl friend. I like Lisa Franklin. I hope they make up."

"Oh . . . is . . . was Lisa his girl friend?"

"Yes — for a long time — until they broke up."

"When was that?"

47

"A couple of months ago. But he still calls her. Don't talk to me until I finish writing the message. . . . Tomorrow at 8:30. Okay, I'll tell him." `

"Thank you."

"Good-bye."

# Wednesday night

"**H**ello!"
        "Hello Jim."

"Angie?"

"What happened to you yesterday? I must have talked to your whole family yesterday."

"I'm sorry. My grandmother was sick. My sister and I had to go over and help out. We had to shop for her and help clean up. It took the whole night. I wanted to call you but I didn't know how."

"Maybe I should give you my number. What do you think?"

"I don't know. What do you think?"

"Well, in one way I'd like you to have my

number. But in another way I wouldn't. It's kind of perfect this way. It's like a mystery."

"I think so too. Let's just leave it alone. Let's just keep it the way it is."

"But I was dying to talk to you yesterday. I couldn't wait. They didn't tell me where you were. They didn't tell me anything."

"My mother doesn't talk much. But Ellen never stops."

"She sounded real cute."

"She didn't say anything, did she?"

"What do you mean?"

"She didn't say anything about me, did she?"

"Nothing much. But Jim, I have something to tell you. Something important."

"What is it?"

"It happened yesterday in school. I couldn't wait to tell you. I couldn't wait for it to be night so I could call. And you weren't even home, so I had to wait all day again today."

"What is it, Angie? What happened?"

"He spoke to me."

"He?"

"Jim. Jim McCone."

"Oh, him!"

"Wait till you hear. I was running along the hall to get to P.E. and suddenly there he was. He was standing in front of me. So I just moved off and kept going. He was smiling at me, right at me. He was looking at me and smiling."

"Congratulations!"

"No — wait! So I just kept moving and he yelled after me, 'Hey, Angie, where's the fire?' "

"So what did you say?"

"I didn't say anything."

"So then what happened?"

"Well, nothing happened. But don't you see? He spoke to me."

"Big deal!"

"It is a big deal. You don't know how many girls in this school are dying for him to speak to them. Even if it's just to say, 'Excuse me.' "

"Angie, is that what you couldn't wait to tell me?"

"No, no, that's not the important part. The important part is that I kept right on going. I didn't stop. I didn't answer him. Don't you see, Jim, I just don't care anymore."

"Oh!"

"It's all over, Jim. I don't care about him anymore. I've been nutsy over him ever since I started high school and now I don't care anymore."

"I'm glad."

"It's because of you, Jim. You helped me. I've only known you since last Monday. But you helped me see what a creep he was. If it weren't for you, I'd be licking his feet right now."

"That's wonderful, Angie. A girl like you doesn't need somebody like him. A girl like you needs somebody for real."

"That's right. I don't know what I ever saw in him. It was all on the outside. Because there's nothing inside him. He's shallow and he's not really interested in me. I couldn't really be me around him."

"You have to be true to yourself, Angie. If you have to pretend to be somebody else, it's no good."

"I love to listen to you, Jim. You sound so good and honest. There's no b.s. with you."

"Angie . . . ."

"What, Jim?"

"Nothing."

"Can I ask you something, Jim?"

"Sure, Angie."

"Have you got a girl friend?"

"No."

"Did you ever?"

"Yes, I did."

"I bet you've had lots."

"I've had . . . some. But now I'm busy with my music. I don't have the time."

"That's too bad."

"What is?"

"That you think a girl friend would interfere with your music. If she was the right kind of person, she could help you. I mean, she could encourage you."

"Yes, if she was the right kind of person."

"Tell me about them."

"About who?"

"About your old girl friends."

"There's not much to tell."

"Tell me about the last one. What was she like?"

"She . . . she . . . was a nice girl."

"Come on, Jim, I've told you a lot about

me, and you've never told me anything about you. What was she like?"

"Well, she was all right. But she kept nagging me all the time. She wanted to do lots of things I wasn't interested in."

"Like what?"

"Like movies. She always wanted to go to the movies."

"What else?"

"She never left me alone. She wanted me to be with her all the time. I need my own space. I need time to work on my music. I can't be crowded."

"No, of course not. So what happened? Did she break it off?"

"No, it was me. 'Forget it!' I told her. I should have told her earlier but I felt sorry for her. I didn't want to hurt her."

"You're a very kind person."

"Well, she wasn't a bad kid. I told her. I said, 'Lis —' I mean, I told her, 'You're a good kid and you just need somebody different from me.'"

"Was she upset?"

"Well sure she was upset."

"Did she ask you not to break it up? To try another time?"

"Yes, she did. She didn't want to end it. She wanted another chance. She said if I gave her another chance she'd change."

"Oh — she really cared for you."

"I guess she did. She . . . she cried. She . . . begged me not to break it up. I tried to explain to her that it was no good for her either. That we just weren't good for each other. That she had to be herself too. She couldn't go changing herself around just for me. Nobody should do that. I don't care who it's for."

"But didn't you feel bad? I mean, for her?"

"Of course I felt bad. You don't stop caring for somebody just because you end a relationship. I told her that. I told her I'd always care for her. I told her I'd always be her friend. I even wrote a song for her."

"You did? Can I hear it?"

"Why not? If you're really interested, I don't mind."

"Go ahead, Jim. Go ahead."

He put down the receiver. She could hear him getting his guitar ready. She could hear

him tuning the strings. Getting ready to sing
to her.

"Are you ready, Angie?"

"I'm ready, Jim."

"Here it is."

> You don't stop caring
> When it's through;
> You don't stop caring
> Me for you.

> No, no, no
> I tell you true,
> You don't stop caring
> Because it's through.

> I'll think of you
> And love you still
> Though we're all burned out
> And over the hill.

> No, no, no
> I tell you true,
> You don't stop caring
> Because it's through.

"God, that's beautiful," she told him. "It's so sad and so beautiful. I think if it was me — I mean if somebody broke off with me, I think I'd feel so proud if he wrote a song just for me. I mean, you can live your whole life without anybody writing a song for you — just for you. But it's such a sad song. Do you always write sad songs, Jim? Don't you ever write songs that are happy?"

"Listen Angie."

> I wake up each morning
> And reach for the sun;
> Got you in my heart
> And my day's work is done.
>
> You're the rose on the stem
> And the bird in the nest,
> You're the world spinning round,
> You're the one I love best.

It was such a bouncy song she couldn't help smiling.

"That's just great, Jim. I love it."

"It's a new one, Angie. I wrote it over the weekend."

57

"No kidding?"

"No kidding. I was feeling pretty good this weekend. That's why I wrote the song."

"Why were you feeling so good, Jim?"

"I'll tell you another time, Angie."

"When?"

"I don't know."

"Tomorrow?"

"Maybe."

"I can't wait until tomorrow."

"Good night, Angie."

"Good night, Jim."

# Thursday night

"**H**ello!"

"Hello Jim."

"Hi Angie. You're right on time. It's exactly 8:30."

"I have 8:32 on my clock. I waited until two minutes after 8:30 so you wouldn't think I was too anxious."

"I wouldn't think that, Angie. Especially since I've been sitting here since a quarter after eight. I didn't want anybody else to get the phone when you called. I was afraid somebody else might call and tie up the line."

"I'd keep calling until it was free."

"That's good."

"Where are you, Jim?"

"I'm at home, naturally."

"No, I mean tell me what it looks like where you are. I want to know what it looks like."

"Well, I'm in my room. It's not really my room. I share it with my brother."

"Tell me what it looks like. Don't leave anything out. I don't want you to leave anything out."

"Okay. I'm sitting on my bed."

"What does it look like?"

"It's just an ordinary bed."

"What kind of a bedspread?"

"No bedspread. I have a red blanket on my bed."

"What kind of sheets?"

"Oh, Angie."

"Come on. I want to know everything."

"Well, they're old sheets. Just ordinary sheets — sort of blue. Kind of old looking."

"Go on."

"Let's see. My brother has a bed with a blue blanket. He's got a desk and I've got a desk. He's got baseball stuff all over his side of the room — banners — you know, for the San Francisco Giants and some of the other teams."

"Like who?"

"You really want to know?"

"Everything. I want to know what it looks like around you."

"Okay. But then you have to tell me what it looks like in your room."

"I was hoping you would ask me. I even cleaned up my room. Anyway, go on. What other teams?"

"Let me see. I hate baseball and I never noticed. He's got an Oakland A's banner, a Cincinnati Reds banner, an L.A. Dodgers banner, a Boston Red Sox banner, and some pictures of players."

"Like who?"

"Like Johnny Bench, George Foster, Vida Blue, and let's see — who's that one — oh, Willie McCovey."

"Okay. What else?"

"Well on my side of the room, I've got posters of some of my favorite performers."

"Like who?"

"Like Elton John, Fleetwood Mac, Linda Ronstadt."

"Do you think she's pretty?"

"Do I ever!"

"Do you think Olivia Newton-John's pretty?"

"She's gorgeous."

"I think so too. Did you see her in 'Grease'? I was crazy about 'Grease.' "

"Yes I saw it."

"What did you think of the music?"

"Only so-so."

"John Travolta was really great."

"He can't sing at all."

"He doesn't have to sing. But go ahead. What else?"

"Nothing else. Some curtains."

"What color?"

"Blue mostly. Blue boats. My mother made them for us when we were kids. They're old."

"What's on the floor?"

"Blue rug — covers the whole floor. Okay. Now it's my turn. What does your room look like?"

"It's kind of small but pretty. I'm in it by myself."

"You've got your own room?"

"Because it's so small. Pat and Dinah share a great big room. I'd rather be by myself even if it is so small."

"So what's in it?"

"Me — to start with."

"Ha, ha, ha!"

"And lots of lips."

"Lips?"

"Uh huh. I save lips. I have eight lips pillows. My friends always try to give me something with lips on it for Christmas or my birthday. Four of the pillows are just red lips. Two of them are red lips with white teeth. And two of them are pink lips."

"That's a funny thing to save."

"See, you don't know anything about me."

"Go on. Go on."

"I have two posters of lips. One is smoking a cigarette and the lips are forming an **O**. The other one is puckered up for kissing. I have a white lips flowerpot with a plant in it. And I have two lips pins. One is pink and the other is red. One is smiling and one is sad. Sometimes I wear them together. Then my curtains are black and white with red lips. I made them myself, and my bedspread is solid pink with no lips. I also have a poster of John Travolta. He's got great lips. I don't know if you ever noticed."

"No, I never did."

"And a poster of a baby tiger cub."

"What kind of lips does he have?"

"And I've got a desk and a chair and a tiny chest. That's all the room there is in here. And there's a red carpet on the floor. It's real pretty. You should see it."

"I wonder if I ever will."

"That's what I wanted to talk to you about."

"Angie."

"What?"

"I wrote another song last night. After we hung up."

"Are you going to sing it, Jim?"

"If you want to hear it."

"I always want to hear your songs."

"Just stay right there, Angie. I'm just reaching out for my guitar."

This time her heart was beating very hard.

She knew something was going to happen. She didn't know what but she knew it was going to be something special. He began to play softly.

> I feel the touch of your fingers
> In the sound of your voice,
> And the beauty of your words
> Lets my heart rejoice.
>
> Your voice in the night
> Has shown me the day;
> Your words stroke my face
> Like the sunshine in May.
>
> Your face may be hidden
> But what's that to me?
> I love only one girl
> And her name is Angie.

When he finished he waited for her to speak, but she remained silent.

"Angie."

"What, Jim?"

"I wrote it for you, Angie. It's your song. I'm calling it 'Angie's Song.'"

"Nobody ever wrote a song to me before.

And what a song! I never heard such a beautiful song."

"And I mean it, Angie. I mean what it says."

"I'm glad, Jim, because . . . because that's the way I feel about you, too."

"It's crazy, isn't it? It's not even two weeks and we don't really know each other."

"Yes we do, Jim. We really do know each other. I feel I know you much better than any other boy I've ever met."

"Oh Angie, what will we do?"

"What we have to do, Jim. We have to meet."

"No, we don't have to meet! No, we mustn't!"

"Why not?"

"Because it wouldn't be right. We have to keep it this way. We don't want anything to spoil it. We don't want anything to change."

"Nothing will change. It will only be better."

"No! No!"

"Don't be so upset, Jim. Why are you so upset?"

"Let's just say good-night now, Angie. I have to work this out. But I love you, Angie. I really do."

"I love you too, Jim. You'll see. It will work out."

"Good night, Angie."

"Good night, Jim."

# Friday night

"**H**ello Angie!"
"Hello Jim."
"Hello."
"Hello."
"I've been thinking about you."
"I've been thinking about you, too."
"What have you been thinking?"
"No, tell me what you've been thinking, Jim."
"I asked you first, Angie."
"Okay, I'll tell you what I've been thinking. I've been thinking how lucky I am. L-U-C-K-Y. I've been writing it all over the

place. I even wrote it on the bathroom mirror this morning in lipstick. L-U-C-K-Y. That's me. Here I call a wrong number and find you at the other end. It could have been anybody but it was you."

"And what about me? Look what happened to me. I found you. I didn't do anything. I wasn't even looking. I was just sitting at home doing nothing and the phone rang. And there you were."

"I never want it to end, Jim."

"Me either, Angie. I want us to go on like this forever and ever and ever."

"But Jim . . . ."

"No, don't say anything. Let me finish. I've been thinking about us. I think we have it made. It's perfect the way it is. Let's keep it that way."

"But Jim, maybe it can be better."

"How can it be better?"

"Because it's only the beginning. I mean, we know a lot about each other. Sometimes you go around with somebody for months and months and you never find out anything about him. Maybe you like the way he looks or the way he dances or the way he dresses. But you don't know how he is inside. With us, we started backward. We know each other inside. We know a lot about each other. Now it will be easy."

"No, it won't."

"Why not, Jim? We can be together. Really together. We can meet each other after classes. We can eat lunch together. We can sit and talk and . . . well . . . we can be together."

"No, no!"

"We can't go on like this forever, Jim."

"No — maybe not forever. But for a while, Angie. Let's not change it for a while."

"I don't see why not, Jim. Unless you . . . you . . . ."

"What?"

"Unless you think you'd be ashamed of me. Is that it, Jim? You think you'd be ashamed of me?"

"Ashamed of you?"

"Because I'm so small and maybe not up to you. Maybe you'd be ashamed of me. Maybe you wouldn't want your friends to see me."

"Oh Angie, that's not it at all. If you only knew."

70

"I think I want to say good-night now, Jim."

"Don't go, Angie. Wait a minute."

"No. I want to say good-night."

"You're crying, Angie. Listen to me."

"Good night, Jim."

"Angie! Angie! Wait Angie!"

# Monday night

"**H**ello!"

"Hello Jim."

"Angie, how could you be so mean? I've been sitting near the phone all weekend waiting for you to call."

"I had to do some thinking, Jim. I needed a little time."

"Angie . . . . "

"Wait. Let me tell you what I've been thinking. I've been thinking that for two people in love we sure have been making each other feel lousy."

"It's my fault."

"Well, I don't know whose fault it is, and

maybe I don't care. I love you, Jim, and I don't want to lose you."

"I love you too, Angie."

"So let's just keep going. Let's not push too hard. If you want to wait awhile, I guess I can go along with it. I don't understand why — maybe I think I do — but anyway, I'm willing to wait."

"Angie, I've missed you so."

"I missed you too. That's why I decided I just can't go on without you. I tried. I went dancing with my friends both Saturday and Sunday. I stayed out of the house. I went shopping Saturday. I bought another lips pin. Now I have three. Sunday afternoon I went skating in the park. I laughed a lot and kidded around with my friends. But I don't know when I had a lousier weekend."

"Just give me a little more time, Angie. There are some things I have to tell you first. It might make a difference."

"Nothing you can say will make a difference."

"Maybe it will. Maybe you'll find out some things about me that you won't like. Maybe you'll be surprised."

"Sure I might be surprised. Lots of things I still don't know about you, but it's not going to make any difference. What I know about you I love — the way you look, your honesty, and your songs."

"Suppose . . . suppose . . . I don't know how I can tell you, but . . . suppose I didn't write songs."

"It wouldn't be you."

"Suppose . . . suppose . . . suppose I wasn't honest. Suppose there were things about me I didn't tell you."

"Nobody's perfect, Jim. You said it yourself."

"But Angie, there are a lot of things about me that aren't perfect."

"About me too. About everybody. You know, you have to look at other people to see who really has problems. Let me tell you something. Today I felt like really dressing up. I wore my three lips pins right across my bright red sweater. It was something else. Maybe something too much because this funny-looking boy started following me. He just stopped short when he saw me in the hall. He even asked a kid in the class, Julie Burns, who I was. I thought to myself, I sure hope I don't have him trailing me."

"Maybe he wasn't trailing you."

"He was."

"You had a good look at him?"

"Enough, I can tell you that. He was a creepy little guy with a big nose. What a contrast with you! That's what I'm telling you. No matter what kind of problems you have, just think of that little, creepy-looking kid. You'll feel better."

"I do think of him, Angie. I think of him a lot."

"What do you mean?"

"Well, how do you know what kind of a person he is, Angie? How do you know he isn't a wonderful person inside?"

"I don't want to know."

"But that's silly and shallow. You should know better. Here you've been trailing Jim McCone for years just because he's so good-looking. You wasted your time. What is he inside? What does he know about other people — about their feelings and their dreams? He's a nothing inside. Maybe that funny-looking little guy with the big nose is beautiful inside.

Maybe you'd really like him if you got to know him. Maybe he's a poet. Maybe he's . . . ."

"Maybe I don't care about him. Maybe I only care about you, Jim. You're the one I want to talk about. Tell me, Jim, what are you so worried about? You have everything going for you. What is it?"

"I can't tell you, Angie. Not now I can't."

"Why not? Maybe I can help you."

"I don't think you can. I think you'd hate me if you knew the truth about me."

"What truth? Are you a murderer? Or what? Oh . . . my God . . . is that it? Are you gay?"

"Are you crazy?"

"Thank goodness it's not that. Are you laughing, Jim? Great! You're laughing."

She started laughing too. Both of them were laughing.

"You're funny, Angie."

"It's better to feel good than to feel bad."

"You're right."

"So let's just feel good. We're so lucky. We have each other. It will all work out. You'll see."

"I guess it will. But let me jusk ask you one question, Angie. Suppose I was different. Suppose I didn't look the way I do. Suppose I didn't write songs. Suppose . . . ."

"It wouldn't be you, Jim. I love you just the way you are, Jim."

"Okay, Angie. Let's just leave it that way then."

"And let's feel good. Okay, Jim?"

"Okay, Angie."

"Good night, Jim."

"Good night, Angie."

# Tuesday night

"Hello!"

"Hello. Is Jim there?"

"Just a minute, please. He's eating dinner."

"I'm sorry to disturb you. I promise I won't talk to him long."

"Hello?"

"Hello, Jim darling. It's me."

"Angie. You're early."

"I can't talk too long tonight. It's my mother's birthday and we're all going out to dinner and a movie."

"How will I ever get through this evening?"

"Maybe I'll try to sneak in a quickie call later. Jim, did anybody ever tell you that you have the most gorgeous voice of any male alive?"

"Uh huh."

"Who? I'll kill her."

"You did."

"That's all right then. What are you eating?"

"Fish."

"Yuk! I hate fish."

"How can you hate fish?"

"It's easy. How can you like it? Is that your mother yelling?"

"No, I think it's the foghorn blowing."

"Funny boy! I better go."

"No."

"I'll call later."

"Promise?"

"Promise. Here's a kiss to tide you over."

"Mmm!"

"Bye, Jim."

"Bye, Angie."

# Tuesday night —
## later

"Hello!"

"Hello Jim."

"Hi, Angie. Where are you?"

"In the movie theater. It's a wonderful movie. Dustin Hoffman is in it. I like him even though he's kind of funny looking."

"Why do you keep harping on looks?"

"Do I?"

"Yes you do. Looks aren't everything."

"No, not everything. You're right. Anyway, the movie is really sad. I hope it turns out okay. I like happy endings."

"So do I."

"I'm glad, Jim, because I know you and me — we're going to have a happy ending."

"We've sure had a wonderful, happy beginning, Angie, haven't we?"

"We sure have. I've got to go now. Good night, darling. Good night, Jim."

"Good night, Angie."

# Thursday evening

"Hello!"
 "Hello."
 "Angie?"
 No answer.
 "Angie, is that you?"
 No answer.
 "Angie, I know it's you."
 "Yeah. It's me."
 "Were you sick yesterday, Angie? Is that why you didn't call? I figured maybe you were sick."
 "No, I wasn't sick."
 "So what happened to you, Angie? I've been sitting by the phone, worrying. Why didn't you call yesterday?"

"I didn't feel like it."

"Why not? What happened yesterday? Your voice — it sounds so funny."

"Your voice doesn't sound funny, Jim. It sounds just the way it always sounds. A little nervous maybe, but it's the same deep, gorgeous voice."

"Something's wrong. I can hear it. Angie, what is it? What's wrong?"

"It's not always easy to hear what's wrong in a voice. Sometimes a voice can fool you. Sometimes you could swear a voice is telling you the truth, for instance. It's funny, Jim, how a voice can fool you. Even a deep, gorgeous voice like yours."

"Angie . . . listen to me, Angie. Before you say anything else let me tell you something about me. Angie, I've been wanting to tell you for a long time."

"No, Jim, it's too late. I want to tell you what happened to me yesterday. That will explain why I didn't call you last night. Don't you want to know, Jim? Don't you want to know what happened to me yesterday?"

"I'm not sure I do."

"Well, I'll tell you anyway. You know that

funny-looking little guy I told you about — the one with . . . ."

"The one with the big nose? Yes, I remember."

"Well, he was there yesterday — outside my typing class this time. He acted like he didn't see me when I came out. He hurried away when I came out. But I knew he had followed me there. Are you listening, Jim?"

"I'm listening."

"I guess I said something to my friend, Sharon, and I guess we were laughing. I asked if she knew who he was. She said no. But there was another girl there, named Lisa Franklin. She saw him too. She said she knew who he was. Do you know her, Jim? A girl named Lisa Franklin?"

"I know her."

"Well, she knew who he was. She said he used to be her boyfriend. She got kind of mad at us for laughing at him. She said it was mean to laugh at people who couldn't help themselves. She said he couldn't help looking funny because of . . . because of . . . ."

"Because of his nose. Go on."

"She seemed like a nice girl."

"She is. She's a very nice girl."

"And not bad looking either. Her skin isn't so good, but she has a nice smile."

"Go on."

"She came and had lunch with us. I never really talked to her before but there was something familiar about her. At first, I didn't know what it was. She told us about him — her old boyfriend. It was hard not to laugh. Some of the things she told us were so funny that I thought I'd burst."

"Look, why don't we just stop right now?"

"No. Let me finish!"

"Go ahead. Get it out of your system."

"He sounded like such a loser. She knew him ever since third grade. Their mothers were friends. They used to play together when they were little. Even then, she was sorry for him. She wouldn't let people pick on him. She said Jim McCone was the worst. He'd tease him and laugh at him because of . . . because of . . . ."

"His nose. Say it, Angie, his nose."

"Yeah, his nose. Well, she felt so sorry for

him that she let him talk her into becoming his girl friend. She didn't want to. She had plenty of friends but he didn't. He was very shy. He didn't have any friends. He was very lonely. He wanted to be with her all the time. He never gave her any peace."

"Is that what she said?"

"That's what she said. I don't think she's lying, either."

"No. She's not lying."

"Finally she told him she needed room. He begged her not to break it up. He said he would change. But she told him it wasn't good for him either. He needed new friends and he had to find his own way. Does that sound familiar, Jim? Jim, are you listening?"

"I'm listening."

"And all the time she was talking, I kept thinking there was something familiar. I didn't put it all together until the end. When she said she thought he was talented. She said he sang and he wrote his own songs. But she said he never sang them to her. She said that he was too shy even to sing them to her. She told him maybe he needed confidence. Maybe it wasn't good for him to have a girl friend he couldn't even sing his songs to."

"She was right."

"That's when I remembered — when she started talking about the songs. I said to her, 'What's your name again?' She said, 'Lisa Franklin.' That's when I remembered."

"Remembered what?"

"What it was I forgot. It was her name. Your little sister told me her name. The night you were away. Your little sister told me your old girl friend's name was Lisa Franklin."

"You're some detective."

"So I said to her, 'What was his name — your old boyfriend?' And she said . . . ."

"His name is Jim Holman."

"I couldn't believe it. But I knew it was true. I had to get up and run away from there or I would have burst out crying. I even went home. I cut my classes and went home. Nobody was home. I cried all afternoon and all evening. My mother thought I was sick. I told her I wasn't. But I couldn't tell her the truth."

"Angie, I'm sorry."

"Oh, that's just great. You think you can

say you're sorry with that great voice of yours and it will be all fine again."

"No, I don't think that."

"You really made an idiot out of me. Boy, was I ever a jerk to fall for that line. But why did you do it? You didn't have to do it. I told you the truth. I never lied to you. Why did you lie to me? Why did you do it?"

"Angie, I'm sorry."

"And I bet you never told Jim McCone off either."

"No. I never did."

"And I bet you're not a pro, are you? A guy who's too shy to even sing his songs to his own girl friend."

"No. I'm not a pro. I'm even too chicken to try out for the chorus."

"Gets better and better all the time. Why should you be too shy to try out for the chorus? You've got a marvelous voice. The one thing you've got is a marvelous voice."

"With you maybe. Not with anyone else. Maybe that's why I wanted you to think I was somebody special. I didn't want you to be sorry for me. At first, it was just fun to talk to you because you didn't know me. But later, when I started really caring about you, I didn't think you could love me the way I am. I guess I knew it couldn't last. But it was wonderful. It was the happiest time in my whole life."

"In mine too. I could really be honest with you. It's funny — all the time you were lying to me, I was being honest with you."

"In a way, I was being honest with you, too. I was letting you see what I really wanted to be. What I wished I was. You're the only one I ever sang my songs to."

"How come you never sang them to Lisa?"

"I guess because I knew she was sorry for me. I thought she'd say they were good even if they weren't. Because she felt sorry for me."

"They are good. They're great."

"I could sing them for you because I knew you weren't sorry for me. I knew you'd tell me the truth. Angie, I've been trying to tell you the truth about me. But I couldn't. And yesterday, outside your typing class, I thought maybe I could talk to you. I didn't know Lisa was in the class. When I saw her, I ran away. Not because of you. I ran away because of her."

"Why should you run away because of her?

Why should you be afraid of her? She's not your girl friend anymore. You don't owe her anything."

"She's a nice girl."

"Maybe she is, and maybe she isn't."

"What do you mean?"

"If she was really a nice girl, she would have made you feel better. You would have been able to sing her your songs. But she felt sorry for you. What right did she have to feel sorry for you? But you knew she felt sorry for you. It made you act silly. The way I always act. The way I always used to act until . . . until I began talking to you."

"It's not her fault. It's mine."

"Anyway, I cried all day yesterday. Today, I just felt mad. At first I wasn't going to call you ever again. But then I thought I would. I thought I would call you and tell you off."

"Go ahead. You have a right."

"I sure do."

"So go ahead."

"Well, what's the use? I guess you couldn't help yourself. I guess you didn't mean to lie."

"Angie, you know I didn't. You know I

wouldn't want to hurt you. The last thing I would ever want to do is hurt you. Do you believe me?"

"I don't know."

"Angie, I swear to you."

"I can't trust you anymore. But what difference does it make anyway? I'm never going to be talking to you again."

"That's right. My God, that's right!"

"So there's no point in swearing or fighting. Let's just forget it ever happened."

"I'll never forget it, Angie."

"I guess I never will either, Jim. I'll never forget your songs. That's right — your songs. Listen, Jim. Listen, stupid. Do something about your songs. They are beautiful songs. You have to do something about them."

"I don't know, Angie."

"I do. You try out for the chorus. Do you hear me? You start out there. Once you get used to standing on the stage, you'll get over your shyness. Then you can do solo numbers. Then maybe you can go pro. You can do it, Jim. Promise me you'll do it."

"I promise."

"Well, that's all then. I guess this is good-bye."

"I'm sorry, Angie."

"So am I."

"Good-bye, Angie."

"Good-bye, Jim."

# Saturday morning– about 2 A.M.

"**H**ello!"
    "Hello Angie."

"You still up?"

"Are you kidding!"

"I don't think I'm going to sleep all night."

"Me either. Isn't it funny, Angie, me calling you?"

"I don't know if I like it."

"Well, you better get used to it."

"Mmm."

"You sound hoarse, Angie."

"So do you, Jim."

"Well, after talking for nearly nine hours straight, I guess it's a miracle either one of us still has a voice left."

"I don't know, Jim, I think with you and me — our voices will never stop. Even after we're dead, our voices will go on."

"We're never going to die, Angie."

"That's the way I feel too, Jim. You know something?"

"What?"

"I knew you'd be waiting for me outside my typing class Friday."

"I knew you knew I would."

"I loved the way you said, 'Hi!' to Lisa. The way you looked right at her and smiled. You've got a nice smile, Jim."

"You've got a nice smile, too."

"And you've got nice bright blue eyes, too. Blue eyes, like you said, and your hair is — well, sort of blond."

"And my nose is sort of big."

"We won't talk about your nose."

"What will we talk about?"

"About you and me. About how we talked all afternoon and all evening. How they had to throw us out of the pizza place, and later how my mom had to throw you out of here because it was so late. How we talked and talked and talked and talked . . . ."

"And checked out your lips collection. You've really got some great lips, Angie."

"You know something, Jim?"

"What, Angie?"

"I think I love you, Jim."

"Listen Angie. There's one other thing I have to tell you."

"You robbed a bank."

"No."

"You murdered your father."

"No — but it's not a bad idea. Listen. I just have to clear up one other thing."

"What is it?"

"You remember I told you my birthday was in October?"

"That's right, October. Are you a Libra or a Scorpio? I forgot to ask you tonight. I'm an Aries."

"Well, it's just that I didn't exactly tell you the truth."

"I hope you're not a Gemini. I hate Geminis."

"No, my birthday really is October 7."

"Libra. That's all right then."

"But I told you I was seventeen. I'm not. I'm sixteen."

"You mean I'm going to be seventeen first?"

"I guess so."

"You mean I'm older than you?"

"Yes. Seven months older. It means I'm going around with an older woman."

"And it means I'm robbing the cradle."

"You don't mind?"

"I do but I'll get used to it."

"What are we going to do tomorrow? I mean today."

"Let's have a picnic in the park. We can go rowing or skating, and then at night, we can go dancing. Jim, do you like dancing?"

"Guess what, Angie?"

"I know. I know. You never went."

"Smart girl!"

"But you'll learn."

"Do I have to?"

"Sure. It'll do you good. Teach you not to shuffle your feet when you're up there on the stage. . . . When you become a great rock star, you have to know how to move. I'll bet you're a natural."

"A natural what?"

She never answered his question. He could hear a loud rap on her door. He could also hear an angry voice. When she spoke, her voice was very low.

"I guess I'll have to say good-night, Jim."

"Was that your mother, Angie?"

"No, my father."

"Does he know it's me?"

"I'm afraid he does."

"I guess he's not going to like me very much."

"I guess not."

"What can I do to get him to like me?"

"Stay off the phone."

"Doesn't look too good."

"I love you, Jim."

"I love you, Angie."

"See you at noon."

"See you then."

"Good night, Jim."

"Good night, Angie."

## About the Author

As a child, Marilyn Sachs decided that the only thing better than reading a good book would be to write one. But what do you write about? After growing up in the Bronx, New York, attending Hunter College in New York City, and working for 10 years as a children's librarian, Marilyn Sachs was ready to write. Since then, she has become a respected and prolific author of children's books.

She and her family now live in San Francisco. Her husband, Morris, is a sculptor, and her two children, Anne and Paul, are college students.